Millions of Americans remember Dick and Jane (and Sally and Spot too!). The little stories with their simple vocabulary words and warmly rendered illustrations were a hallmark of American education in the 1950s and 1960s.

But the first Dick and Jane stories actually appeared much earlier—in the Scott Foresman Elson Basic Reader Pre-Primer, copyright 1930. These books featured short, upbeat, and highly readable stories for children. The pages were filled with colorful characters and large, easy-to-read Century Schoolbook typeface. There were fun adventures around every corner of Dick and Jane's world.

Generations of American children learned to read with Dick and Jane, and many still cherish the memory of reading the simple stories on their own. Today, Pearson Scott Foresman remains committed to helping all children learn to read—and love to read. As part of Pearson Education, the world's largest educational publisher, Pearson Scott Foresman is honored to reissue these classic Dick and Jane stories, with Grosset & Dunlap, a division of Penguin Young Readers Group. Reading has always been at the heart of everything we do, and we sincerely hope that reading is an important part of your life too.

Dick and Jane is a registered trademark of Addison-Wesley Educational Publishers, Inc.
From THE NEW WE LOOK AND SEE. Copyright © 1956 by Scott Foresman and Company,
copyright renewed 1984. From THE NEW WE WORK AND PLAY. Copyright © 1956 by Scott
Foresman and Company, copyright renewed 1984. From THE NEW WE COME AND GO.
Copyright © 1956 by Scott Foresman and Company, copyright renewed 1984. All rights
reserved. Published by Grosset & Dunlap, a division of Penguin Young Readers Group,
345 Hudson Street, New York, NY, 10014. GROSSET & DUNLAP is a trademark of Penguin
Group (USA) Inc. Published simultaneously in Canada. Printed in the U.S.A.

Library of Congress Cataloging-in-Publication Data is available.

ISBN 0-448-43405-9 (pbk)   C D E F G H I J

ISBN 0-448-43417-2 (GB)   B C D E F G H I J

JE Reader
Dick

Read with

Dick and Jane

Go, Go, Go

GROSSET & DUNLAP • NEW YORK

Table of Contents

Go, Go, Go

Come, Spot.
Come and go.
Jump, jump.
Jump up, Spot.
Jump up.

Oh, Jane.

Look and see.

See Sally go.

See Tim go.

See Spot and Puff go.

Oh, Dick.

Look and see.

See Spot jump down.

See Puff jump down.

Down, down, down.

Oh, oh, oh.

Come

Come, Sally.
Come, come.

Oh, Sally.

Come, come.

Come, Sally, come.

Oh, see.
See Sally go.

Go, Sally, go.
Go, go, go.

See Jane Go

Oh, Sally.

See Jane go down.

Down, down, down.

See Jane go down.

Look, Jane.
Look, look.
Oh, look.

Look, Tim, look.

Oh, look.

See funny, funny Jane.

See funny Jane go.

Sally and Mother

Sally said, "Oh, see.
See Mother go.
Come, Dick.
Come, Jane.
Come and go."

Jane said, "Oh, Dick.
See Sally and Tim.
Oh, oh, oh.
See Baby Sally go.
Go, Dick, go."

Sally said, "Oh, Mother.

See Dick go down.

See Jane go down.

Funny, funny Dick and Jane."

The Boats Go

Oh, Dick.

The blue boat can go.

The yellow boat can go.

My little red car can go.

Look, look.

See my red car go.

Oh, oh.

See my red car.

See my red car go down.

Down, down, down.

Oh, Dick.

Help, help.

My little red car is down.

Up, up, up.

Up comes the little red car.

Look, Baby Sally.

See Dick help.

See the little red car come up.

Up, up, up.

The little red car is up.

The Big Red Boat

Come, Baby Sally.

Come and see Father work.

See Father make boats.

Look, Sally.

The little boat is my boat.

I can make my boat blue.

See my little blue boat.

Look, Sally, look.

See my big boat.

I can make my boat red.

Look, Sally.

See my boat.

See my big red boat.

Oh, look, look.

See Puff jump.

See my boat go down.

Oh, look.

My boat is yellow.